# Mayan and The Legion of Alice
## by Steve Hart

I0584514

It's not hard to imagine that corporations can have more money, power and influence than governments.

For elected representatives to put the interests of their financial backers ahead of the people who voted for them.

For politicians to turn a blind eye to the obvious imbalance in a financial system that allows private organisations to create the money a country needs to keep its economic wheels turning.

And to knowingly prevent change that would benefit all its citizens above a handful of interested parties in the banking industry.

To ignore the facts in favour of feathering their own nest, so as to smooth their way from public service to private wealth.

Mayan and The Legion of Alice

## COPYRIGHT

A catalogue record of this book is available at the New Zealand National Library.

Paperback ISBN: 978-0-473-48557-3
Audio book ISBN:  978-0-473-48560-3
Kindle ISBN:  978-0-473-48558-0
PDF: 978-0-473-48559-7

The moral right of the author to be associated with this work has been asserted.
First edition: July 2019

Written and Published by Steve Hart
Illustrations: Andrew Louis

Steve Hart, PO Box 300505, Albany, Auckland, 0752.

# Mayan and The Legion of Alice

www.SteveHart.co.nz

# Mayan and The Legion of Alice

# Chapter 1
## The journey home

Having spent months lying low on Mars, Mayan Levantis was looking forward to returning to Earth. She had tired of Dorado, the only city on Mars, and was keen to stand on her own planet once again.

Yes, Earth had been ravaged by corporations; all of humanity was under permanent surveillance with few places left to be totally private, and no communication went unchecked thanks to monumental buildings stuffed with eavesdropping supercomputers.

As she put a few belongings into her backpack Mayan thought how odd it was that Mars was still referred to as the Red Planet. Photos from the 20th century showed it with a rusty-coloured surface and a pink atmosphere – but few at the time knew the pictures had been altered to hide its Earth-like terrain, blue sky and white clouds.

Images revealing liquid rivers and flowing oceans on Mars had never been made public.

She would have to be careful returning home after her narrow escape leaving State Europe's Port Merian where a drone had raised the alarm.

Ignoring commands over her radio to stay put she left carrying undocumented cargo – more worried about the crooks who'd hired her than the customs guards with their armed robotic Chasers; four-legged robots that took down anyone who didn't submit.

She hoped that by now the authorities might have forgotten all about her.

Even today she had no idea what she had delivered for Teador, but she got 50,000 credits for her trouble – enough to install new fuel cells and update her ship's navigation software – essential to avoid rock clusters drifting around in space. She had chanced her arm long enough with out of date maps.

Mayan gave one last glance around the white moulded interior of her sleeping booth in one of Dorado's cheaper hotels and caught sight of herself in a mirror.

She stood tall, slim and had thick dark purple hair to below her shoulders. She figured she looked a little older than her 24 years, shrugged, and stepped into the bustling corridor.

Patting her right hip to make sure her G5 Defender was holstered she headed to Hangar 27 where her ship, The Mocolet, was waiting. Her's was a C class ship with seating for five people, four bunks, and a cargo hold.

She made a pretty decent living moving people and goods between Earth, the Moon and Mars. Corporations, smugglers, migrants and...well, anyone with the dough could hire her. Although she did have some rules; no drugs, no alcohol, and most important of all – no freebies.

It was an exploding star creating a new sun that had paved the way for people to settle on Mars centuries ago. Of course some things were different than Earth; which now had two suns. The sky on Mars was slightly more turquoise than blue, a day lasted a little more than 24 hours and a year was 687 days – not that it mattered to most people.

Although annual celebrations were lost to the history books, day 343 was a national holiday on Mars and retailers would have special offers such as buy one (of items no one really needed) to get *three for free.*

Mass consumerism continued on Mars, as it did on Earth, even though it had contributed to the devastation of Earth's natural environment. Lessons, it seemed, would not be learned if there was a chance of profiting from natural resources.

People migrated to Mars wanting a new life away from an overpopulated Earth with its crumbling infrastructure. However, there were now some places on the 'Old World' where it never ever got really dark as a result of having two suns.

There was only one problem for those wanting to relocate to Mars; wannabe migrants had to be free of debt to move beyond their country's borders or leave Earth.

Poverty was so extreme and widespread that parents were handing down their debts to their children. There was little inherited wealth; just inherited debt. The banks owned everything and only the exceptionally privileged had anything like real freedom and liberty.

Yes there had been protests; mass protests. But a combination of brute-force by military police, armed drones and Chasers that would hunt down protest leaders, had all but quelled further revolts.

Debt slavery was rife across the planet thanks to hundreds of years of banks calling the shots; telling governments how to run their countries, controlling employment law, and raising interest rates on a whim to control the populace for corporations who wanted a cheap, subservient, and frightened workforce.

If there was any sign of people getting their debts down; due to some imbalance somewhere in the system, then the banks would whack up interest rates to suck credits out of people's pockets. Strikes were outlawed; as were worker unions.

It was therefore impossible for 99% of people to ever pay off their debts and real freedom and liberty were fanciful thoughts for most. Only the wealthiest enjoyed the fresh air and water on Mars.

As she approached the triple glazed door at Hangar 27 a thin red line flashed down Mayan's face.

"Hello Mayan," said a synthetic voice that was

neither male nor female in tone.

"You have three messages. Shall I copy them to your ship's computer?"

"Go ahead."

The industrial hangar was dim and noisy, but the clang of Mayan's boots on the metal floor cut through the sound of the general hubbub often found at the dirty end of any port. Just 30 metres away was her ship.

"Hey Levantis!"

Mayan rested her hand on the G5, looked down at its handle and saw it was low on power (I knew I should have put it on charge). She turned to see a dark man with a teenage girl.

"Levantis! Remember me?"

"What do you want Carter?" Said Mayan with a hint of suspicion.

"We need a ride. I hear you're on you way to Earth – room for two more on top?

"What's the deal?"

"No deal," said Carter "We had transport arranged with Charbonneau but we're stranded. It's all turned to custard. You seen him?"

Charbonneau owed Mayan two things – credits and an explanation. She couldn't quite decide what she wanted most. Either way, he was going to pay.

"It'll cost ya. No free rides here," said Mayan as she put a foot on the ramp of her ship.

"It's okay," grinned Carter. "We know you ain't no charity. I've got enough for you."

"I want more than enough."

Carter looked furtive. "Say 7,000, to put us down on the Moon?"

"Let's say 12,000 and get aboard now or it'll be 15. You and your silent friend are making me nervous."

Within a few minutes Mayan was looking over her control panel, flicking switches and touching screens to fire up her engine and engage the navigation computer.

"Raise hatch and check the perimeter," she said aloud waiting for the ship to react.

Leaning forward in her chair she pressed a green button, pushed the control stick forward, and her craft started to rise above the floor. As she spun The

Mocolet around to face the exit she glimpsed three guards pointing in her direction holding weapons.

"Whatever they wanted it was too late now," she thought.

Mayan engaged the main thruster and felt a series of blasts hit the rear of her craft. Acceleration was swift and she watched as the city started to disappear from view on a screen.

## Chapter 2

### Mystery girl

Once The Mocolet was on autopilot Mayan searched for her passengers.

"So what's your name?" She said looking directly at the girl; forcing her into a stare.

"It's Trionfi," replied Carter.

"There's food and drink in there, help yourself," said Mayan.

"This your idea of inflight service?"

"It's as good as it gets," snapped Mayan.

"Have you got any fresh drinking water then?" Asked Carter.

"Don't be silly," she said. "But I'll tell you what. When you've finished you can tell me why we were shot at as we left."

Back on the flight deck Mayan put her feet up and leaned back in her chair which had clearly seen better days. It sported strips of odd coloured thick adhesive tape covering tears and holes in the fabric. Yeah it was falling apart, but as far as Mayan was concerned it was the most comfortable chair in the solar system.

"Computer, messages please."

In an instant a screen flickered into life.

"Thanks for the delivery; got another one for you. Teador," read the first.

The next message down said Kane.

"Hi Mayan. Hope you can come home so we can celebrate your birthday. Love Dad."

The last message opened to reveal a screen full of gibberish text and computer code. Mayan asked the computer to decipher it.

"One moment please," it replied in a voice that exuded calmness and was at the same time both monotone and harmonious with a hint of condescension. "This message uses a deprecated encryption program. There is no valid return address."

Carter cleared his throat to announce his presence.

"You've got a great ship here," he smiled.

"What happened to Charbonneau? Who's the girl?" Said Mayan.

"Hey, you got a lot of questions considering we're paying guests," said Carter. "I heard you weren't that fussy. But the last time I saw Charbonneau was in the Mars Bar three days ago."

Mayan was intrigued.

"But what about that trouble just as we left?"

"I wish I knew," he shrugged. "But it's nothing to do with me I'm sure. How long until the Moon?"

"Six hours once the Scram Drive kicks in. The navigation app is updating now."

Carter left for one of the bunks.

"Oh, the girl's asleep," he said.

Mayan returned to her messages.

"Computer, any luck on that gibberish?"

"Still processing Mayan."

She pushed a button on her console and the flight deck slowly filled with ambient dance music.

With the Scram Drive booted up Mayan watched as the stars streamed by; almost looking like a smear with no end. She was now in the hands of her computer to get them to the Moon in one piece.

With her eyes closed a thousand images and thoughts passed through her mind as she fell into a deep sleep. She thought of home, her father, and images of Earth, Mars and the Moon merged into one psychedelic dream. For a moment she thought she could almost smell the scent of a fresh rose. The music faded and the silence brought her back to the job at hand – landing on the Moon.

There were many folk stories of Moon landings centuries ago. But no footprints, flags, landers or Nasa Moon buggies were found when the first settlers arrived. What they did find were structures many thousands of years old.

One was a glass tower six kilometres tall; the other featured a huge radio dish. Few were surprised when Nasa finally admitted what everybody knew – its moon landings in the 1960s and 70s were hoaxed for political reasons.

"Mayan," said the computer. "I have an incoming transmission from Kane."

He appeared on her comms screen sitting at a dining table in his home.

"Hey, you likely to make it to Melbourne? I really need to see you – okay!" He said.

"Who's that standing in the shadow – anyone I

know?" Said Mayan.

"No, just a friend."

Mayan looked hard and paused: "Look I've got to go. I'll see you in about 12 hours."

As Mayan's ship closed in on the Moon she spoke to an operator at Lunar Control.

"This is Mayan Levantis approaching Lunar 4, requesting permission to land. I have two passengers and no cargo, over."

There was a pause, a crackle and then a voice replied: "Okay, confirm the name of your ship and your ID number?"

"The Mocolet; 211242244."

"Switch to external navigation, we'll pull you in," came the response.

When the Moon had become habitable, living in a lunar dome was the next big thing. But almost everyone who moved there regretted it; mainly due to the claustrophobic confinement. They gave it a name; Moon Sickness.

Inside the Lunar 4 hanger Mayan's ship was lightly sprayed with chemicals. Mayan and her passengers entered an airlock where a light scanned them, three doors slid open and each entered a small cubicle. A huge ceiling fan pushed warm air down on them for a few seconds, another door opened and they were free to enter the network of tubes and domes that was Lunar City.

What had started out as a clinical white interior had turned a tarnished grey; grubby with age and want of maintenance. Ceiling lights flickered here and there and outside – through windows inches thick – were hundreds of domes surrounded by a soulless, grey and forbidding landscape.

Still, the stars looked bright and clear above and around the Lunar surface. No twinkling stars here; just bright orbs hanging in the absolute blackness of space.

"Why anyone would want to live here is beyond me," thought Mayan. "Lunar City? More like Lunacy!"

"Where's the bar?" She asked looking at a guard wearing crumpled clothes and scruffy shoes.

He nodded the direction and Mayan was on her way. Clearly Carter and the girl had other plans so

Mayan left hoping to bump into Charbonneau.

The bar was busy but with no sign of her friend she had a drink, unsuccessfully pitched for a gig from one of her regulars who wanted to beat her down on price, and started making her way back to The Mocolet via a fast food joint.

But where was Charbonneau, why had he left Mars without a word? Something else was spinning around Mayan's head – who was that girl?

Mayan headed back to her ship munching on a veggie round – couldn't call them burgers. Within a few minutes she was waiting for clearance to leave the Moon; destination Melbourne, Australia.

Having entered Earth's atmosphere, she called Kane and left a message.

"I don't care what they say," thought Mayan, "there is nothing like Earth."

It was home – dirty, polluted, radiated, poisoned – but it was the only place she could settle.

Landing at her father's home was easy; she'd done it a thousand times before. Then there was a short walk to the front of Kane's house, the door opened, and

Mayan carried on walking without missing a step.

"Anyone here? Dad! I'm home."

She walked into Kane's study where jazz music was blaring out – Bix Beiderbecke the cornet player. She turned the music off to give her head some space to think, but the silence only seemed to increase her anxiety.

Mayan instinctively reached for her gun and pulled it slowly from its holster; its small screen indicated it was fully charged to fire high intensity G5 pulses.

There was movement upstairs, a noise. Mayan ran up the wooden staircase, the souls of her boots touching down on each step perfectly as she bounded to the top. She burst into the first room she saw and sitting on a chair was Charbonneau.

"What the hell are you doing here? Where's my father?"

"I was supposed to meet him but there was no sign when I arrived; but there was another guy here."

"What guy?"

"Teador."

"And where's Teador now?"

"Probably halfway to a place far away from here if he has any sense," said Charbonneau.

"I'm not so sure about that," said Mayan. "Anyway, what are you even doing here – we were supposed to meet on Mars. You just vanished."

"I know," said Charbonneau. "For now though, I think we need to get out of here. Where's the girl – Trionfi?"

Mayan explained she left her on the Moon with Carter.

"Couldn't get a word out of her; the first silent teenager I've ever met," said Mayan.

Charbonneau looked in horror: "No, she has to be with you! That was the whole point - you left her on the Moon? What were you thinking?"

Just before it got really interesting they both stopped to listen to footsteps echoing from downstairs…

"You two; get down here," hollered a voice.

Waiting for them was Teador; tall, grey hair, fit, and wearing his trademark dark glasses – which no one had ever seen him take off.

Holding a surprisingly long machete with a blade

that sparkled as though embossed with freshly cut diamonds he said: "Mayan, at long last...."

She walked down the stairs with Charbonneau two steps behind.

"...Now keep that gun in your holster and you won't lose a hand."

Mayan collected her thoughts, as she looked at Charbonneau over her shoulder and attempted to rationalise what was going down.

Sitting around Kane's dining table, Teador explained that the box Mayan had delivered to his contact on Mars contained an IBM 5100 computer made in 1975. He told them its operating system was so old it could be connected to the One World mainframe without being detected. And from there it could access a back door to the World Bank.

"The computer's rare, just a handful left on the planet, it's a working museum piece," said Teador.

"Stolen then," chipped in Mayan.

"We're just borrowing it, to run a virus program...I need you to get me to an abandoned space station where the 5100 is being hooked up."

"And what if I don't want to?"

Teador looked to the floor, pushed back in his chair, and as he slid his machete back into its dark brown sheath he looked up at Mayan.

"Where's the girl?"

## Chapter 3
## The 5100

Mayan, Charbonneau and Teador sat around a small table fixed to the floor of her ship; thrown together by an obsolete IBM computer that was just the right height to be a talking-piece foot stool in some upmarket penthouse.

Mayan didn't quite know where to start, but before she could utter a syllable Teador explained that the operating system of the 5100 was unique in computing history, it had novel capabilities known to just a few people. It was something that had come to light while Teador was reading archived forums from the early 2000s – a light-bulb moment that led to a chain of events unfolding that now involved Mayan.

He said: "Tarot is a computer virus written by members of the Legion of Alice that will zero everyone's debt and allow people to travel freely once more.

"Not only that, we believe we have a programme that will credit people's accounts with the exact amount they spend – imagine that! No more debt slavery."

"Where's the virus now," asked Mayan.

Teador tapped his breast pocket: "That's why I have to get up there. I made a solemn promise to members of the Legion that I would get it to them."

Even knowing of a computer virus meant life in prison; actually being found with one meant death within hours – summary justice – no trial, no mercy, no appeal.

"I'm not sure I want any part of it," said Mayan.

Teador explained that The Legion of Alice had boarded abandoned space station 784 which was to be sent toward the sun for destruction in a day or two.

The plan was to access the World Bank from the space station and bring corporations to their knees. But time was short.

"We need the girl; she has a photographic memory and knows the 5100's computer language inside out," said Teador. "But given you've lost her we're stuffed."

"Then you don't need me," smirked Mayan.

"But Mayan!" Pleaded Teador as he glanced at a message on his watch. "Even without her we have a chance of getting access and doing some damage.

"This is bigger than any of us; think of what we can do! Remove control of the corporations, kick the banks out of the picture, and bring balance and fairness back to the planet, to society – the people. Our people."

With his voice trembling with emotion and exhaustion Teador said: "This is huge and we are so close...Years of work have gone into this moment and we are on the cusp of achieving so much. The resistance has been working for decades to get humanity out of this living misery.

"You've worked for the corporations, so using you and your ship we can get in and out without a hitch."

Mayan wasn't so sure.

"Well the authorities were on my tail last time I left here carrying your old box of rotten chips and they fired at my ship when I left Mars; so I am not the sure bet you think I am," she said.

Charbonneau interrupted.

"Yes there is a risk, lots of people have taken risks to get us this far. People have died. But we need to get up there within a few hours to have a chance of freeing the people, freeing yourself," he said. "Your dad's debt will one day be your debt; you will never actually own anything because of it. You'll die poor."

"I'll die old though," snipped Mayan.

Charbonneau continued: "You know banks create credits out of thin air, lend them out and charge interest on something that doesn't actually exist. They're just numbers in a corrupt system. Let's reboot the system for all humanity. Anyway, what the hell else you doing today – you got a date?"

Mayan pondered for a moment, stifled a grin, and thought what a rotten birthday it was. There wasn't even a cake.

"So there's no other pilot, no other ship you could use? It's me or nothing; is that what you're saying?"

Teador lifted his dark glasses up and placed them slowly on the table. He looked first at Charbonneau; and then turned to Mayan with his emerald green eyes that seemed to pierce her very soul.

"We just need you to get us up there and then you can go; we can use an emergency pod to get back to Earth if it all works out – all the space stations have them," he said. "How about that? One last ride."

Mayan looked at her phone, something everyone was compelled to carry for identification purposes, and which helpfully displayed the amount of debt she was in. It was a huge number; the debt was crippling and it was only going to get bigger.

"What about Trionfi?" Said Mayan. "Don't we need her for this suicidal plan to work?"

Teador assured her it would be OK; he had a message from Carter.

"Seems the girl is one step ahead of us, she's on station 784 now," said Teador.

"Carter says you made him nervous – someone from the Legion got him and Trionfi to the station. They're waiting for us now. Right now. What do you say?"

## Chapter 4

## Tarot

Flying out of Australia, now officially a State of the old USA – which had changed its name to Camex as it encompassed Canada and Mexico – was easy enough with Mayan flying manually. But her ship would have caused a blip on someone's screen. She only hoped it was a green dot and not a nasty red one. Still, she'd find out soon enough if a Ceptor flew up next to her asking awkward questions.

With all three of them on The Mocolet's flight deck Mayan flew around the planet to a spot above State Europe where space station 784 was held in a geostationary orbit.

It was much bigger than she imagined, and Mayan had a big imagination. The station had been a communications hub, providing instant communication between Earth and the Moon.

Manned by up to 20 people at a time its engineers and comms specialists would ensure voice, video, and data flowed freely between the two locations and

*Andrew Louis*

update systems to stop hackers – mainly corporations – from getting confidential information from government departments.

The station had seen better days and was now at the end of its useful life; but was still a testament to its engineers.

"Before you dock Mayan there's a few things you need to know," said Teador.

Engaging Geo Mode so her craft would move in tandem with the space station 10km away Mayan yawned in the direction of Teador.

"We think it still has Autobots on board."

"Of course it has," said Mayan sarcastically. "I mean why make it easy when we can clamber aboard illegally and have to face machines that will shoot us on sight. I can understand why you might want to keep that nugget of information to yourself until we were knocking on their door."

Charbonneau assured Mayan there was nothing to worry about.

"Found the off switch have we?" She said.

Autobots were brutal machines that were ruthless.

They didn't think, reason, nor forgive those without a badge sporting a chip with a clearance code.

Installed to prevent pirates from boarding space stations they had done a good job. Yes there had been accidents; a wrong code here, a faulty weapon there, but pirates didn't chance their luck any more.

"I'll keep it simple," said Mayan. "We'll dock, you get off and I fly away – how's that sound?"

Teador had to step in again.

"Mayan, you were sent a message featuring lots of code, and your computer probably couldn't work out what it was – yes?"

Teador explained that the gibberish machine code was the Tarot virus; and while it's in a raw state on her computer it is harmless – but once her ship docks with the space station it can transfer the code to the 5100. Once fully downloaded the IBM can form it into a fully-fledged virus app that can be launched to infect the network.

"So I'm sorry to say you can't leave until the deed is done," he said.

"But you said you had the Tarot program in your

pocket," said Mayan.

"I lied."

She stood up, pulled out her G5, flicked a switch on the handle and pointed the nozzle at Teador's head: "Why the hell involve me in all this; why me? I can't believe this – this is just great! Just GREAT!"

Charbonneau moved to stand between them.

"Mayan! You may not realise it but you are a renegade – you are," he shouted. "You help migrants, carry stuff you know you shouldn't, go places that are off limits to people like us, dodge, duck and dive – you're one of us.

"Now just calm down; stick that thing back in your pocket and let's finish this."

Clearly very angry Mayan sat back in her chair and pressed a few buttons on the ship's master control panel.

"I don't want to be here; I want to go home!" She said talking to herself.

And with that she took control of the ship and headed toward the space station. Charbonneau sat beside her, put on a headset and opened up communication with Carter.

"Ready when you are Mayan."

With that she headed toward the station's docking platform and reversed in until her ship clicked into place with a shudder and a clang.

"Okay," she said. "You two head to the back and hopefully your IDs will get you in without any fuss."

"Here's yours," said Teador tossing Mayan a shiny black badge to pin on her belt. "You stay here for now; once we're on board we'll get connected and you can transfer Tarot to the 5100."

"And *then*…" said Mayan with as much sarcasm as she could muster.

"And then," said Charbonneau. "You come and see your dad. Oh, and bring your gun. We might need it."

# Chapter 5
## Deployment

With Tarot copied across to the IBM Mayan deleted the code from her ship's computer and headed to the space station. Heading to the sound of people talking she entered a large room; hot due to failing air conditioning, and an atmosphere of excitement you could cut with a machete.

Tapping away at an old style keyboard almost trance like, and watching characters appear on a green screen monitor, was Trionfi. Looking at her as she navigated her way into the mainframe using pure code was Teador, Carter and Charbonneau. Sitting well out of the way and swigging from a silver metal flask was Kane.

"So this is where you are," said Mayan to her dad.

"Yeah, sorry girl. Things got ahead of me – didn't really mean to involve you. Happy birthday."

"Yeah," she said. "Do you think I'll have another one?"

"Quiet, let Trionfi finish," whispered Carter.

On the corner of a console a red light started flashing.

"That's new," said Carter.

"What is," said Mayan.

"A light, there, flashing."

At the other end of the station an Autobot was flickering into life. Unusual signals from the station to Earth had been detected and a repeater had triggered security.

"They won't believe we're here doing anything legit," said Carter. "This dump is days away from destruction. Someone's onto us."

Trionfi carried on typing until the screen changed from raw code to something like a modern display of familia icons.

"She's in!" Announced Teador.

And with that he eased her out of the chair to start entering a code to enable Tarot. But before he could lay his hands on the keyboard a rumble came from down the corridor.

"Leave it to me," said Kane as he launched himself

from his chair and grabbed a gun off the wall.

Charbonneau joined him as they entered a corridor and prepared themselves for whatever was coming. In the distance came sounds of doors sliding open, the occasional whoosh, a beep, a flash of light. Terror started to build.

"This won't end well," muttered Kane. "Close the door Mayan – you won't want to see this."

And with that she unquestionably slammed the door closed and spun a wheel to lock it.

"Well that's it," she said to no one in particular. "We're stuffed now. Happy?"

Outside Charbonneau and Kane began to edge forward to meet whatever it was that was heading in their direction. Kane fired a blast into the darkness which only gave an Autobot the confirmation it needed on where to go.

"Why the hell did you do that?" Said Charbonneau knowing their fate was now sealed.

There was movement, a bolder sized tin can with a red light and arms like two miniature cranes was coming for them. They both fired and blasted to bring

Andrew Louis

the machine down – but it just kept coming.

Flashes of gun fire lit up the corridor as the Autobot returned shots with the precision of a sniper.

Kane was hit but carried on shooting. Charbonneau pulled him out the way to a side room by his shirt collar with one hand and fired with the other. With just a moment to catch their thoughts, and their breath, the two of them ventured back out to challenge the machine. The cold, relentless, machine.

If they let it get into the control room then it really was game over. Kane took another hit; this time fatal. With nothing left to worry about Charbonneau returned fire using both his and Kane's gun.

He let out a series of rapid fire shots until both guns just clicked – out of power. With no options left he legged it back to the control room and banged on the door.

"I need help," he shouted. "Incoming."

And with that out came Mayan. Pushing Charbonneau to one side in the smoke-filled corridor she blasted the Autobot with a single shot to its head. As it drifted to one side Mayan, choking on the thick air, blasted it again – there was no defence against a G5 power blast.

The Autobot dropped to the floor and started to roll but in a final act killed Charbonneau with a shot to his chest.

Ignoring the horror Mayan pulled her trigger again – a final blast and the Autobot was a gonna. The lights were on, but no one was home.

"Party's over," shouted Mayan as she entered the control room. "There's bound to be another one – and the people downstairs will know there's something up."

"You can bet your sweet treats they know something's up," smiled Teador – his eyes sparkling with the excitement of a job well done.

"Tarot is tearing through the network right now. They won't have a clue what's going down – man I wish I was there to see it. They will be going insane."

Carter looked out the window to point and laugh at Earth, but instead saw stars.

"Something's up," he said. "I think they've released us – we're moving."

"Yes," said Mayan. "Listen, that's an engine. Look at that star chart – we're heading toward the sun."

Carter, Mayan, Trionfi and Teador ran to the airlock to board The Mocolet.

"Wake up computer," shouted Mayan as she entered its flight deck. "Release us from the space station – quickleeee!"

There was a moment's silence while it processed the command.

"I'm sorry," said the computer in its insanely calm tone. "Unable to disengage."

"Teador!" Screamed Mayan. "We have to manually break free. Go to the airlock and use the handle to unhook us or we're all going to cooksville and there's no dessert."

Push, pull and twist as he might, Teador couldn't get the door mechanism to release. Both the space station and the ship were bonded together – a safety feature that was now going to kill them all. There was only one thing for it.

Teador pushed a button and spoke: "Mayan, Carter, it's been fun but there's only one way you guys are going home. So unless you want a real hot date there's only one thing for it. See ya."

And with that he dashed through the airlock, sealed the doors behind him and – taking just a moment to process what he was about to do – yanked on the ship release handle with all his weight.

With a whoosh of air The Mocolet broke free and he watched as it floated away hoping to see its engine light up – confirmation his deed hadn't been wasted. But there was no time for sightseeing, out of the darkness was movement – an Autobot flickered into life – its red light scanning for activity.

"I hope your cooling system's working," said Teador with a grin. "It's gonna get warm."

*The End*